Note to Parents

Animal Antics, Level 1 of the *Now I'm Reading!*™ series, uses a step-by-step approach to introduce the emergent reader to the beginning phonics skills of short-vowel sounds.

Each of these five fun-filled stories will make your child giggle with delight as they practice each short-vowel sound. At the same time, other basic reading skills, such as sight words, consonants, word endings, digraphs, and consonant blends will be reinforced. Story 1 is the easiest and story 5 is the most challenging. For optimum success, have your child read the stories in sequence the first few times. After that, as your child grows more comfortable with the various skills, he or she can read the stories in any order.

For more information on how to use these stories with your child, refer to the pages at the end of this book.

NOW I'M READING!™

ANIMAL ANTICS

LEVEL 1 ▮ VOLUME 1

Written by Nora Gaydos
Illustrated by BB Sams

Hardcover Bind-up Edition
copyright © 2001, 2004 by innovative KIDS®
All rights reserved
Published by innovative KIDS®
A division of innovative USA®, Inc.
18 Ann Street
Norwalk, CT 06854
Printed in China

Conceived, developed and designed
by the creative team at innovative KIDS®
www.innovativekids.com

For permission to use any
part of this publication, contact
innovative KIDS®
Phone: 203-838-6400
Fax: 203-855-5582
E-mail: info@innovativekids.com

Table of Contents

FAT
CAT

Skills in this story: Vowel sound: short *a;* Sight words: *a, is;* Word ending: *-s;*
Initial consonant blends: *cl, gl;* Final consonant blend: *-st*

A cat.

A tan cat.

A tan fat cat.

A tan fat cat ran.

A tan fat cat ran fast.

A tan fat cat is last.

A tan fat cat is sad.

CATS CLAP!

A tan fat cat has pals.

A tan fat cat is glad.

HOT DOG

kills in this story: Vowel sound: short *o;* Sight words: *a, on, in, the;* Word ending: *-s;*
tial consonant blends: *st, fl;* Final consonant blend: *-st*

A dog.

A hot dog.

A hot, hot dog.

A hot dog got on a log.

A hot dog got on a log in the fog.

A hot dog got lost on a log.

A hot dog got lost on a log in the fog

SOB! SOB!

Stop the log!

A hot dog flops off the log.

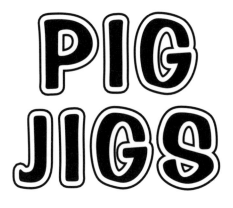

PIG JIGS

Skills in this story: Vowel sound: short *i*; Sight words: *a, and, on, no, the*; Word ending: *-s*; Initial consonant blends: *sl, fl, st*

A pig.

A pig and a wig.

A big pig jigs.

A big pig jigs on a hill.

A big pig jigs on a hill and slips.

A big pig jigs on a hill and slips on a wig.

SLIPS and FLIPS!

A big pig hits his hips.

No jigs!

A big pig sits still on the hill.

RUB-
A-DUB
CUB

Skills in this story: Vowel sound: short *u*; Sight words: *a, in, the, is, on, no;*
Word ending: *-s;* Initial consonant blend: *st;* Final consonant blend: *-mp*

A cub.

A cub dug.

A cub dug up mud.

A cub dug up mud in the sun.

YUCK!

Mud is stuck on the cub.

No fun!

A cub jumps in a tub.

A cub rubs in the suds.

Rub-a-dub-dub!

WET LEGS!

ills in this story: Vowel sound: short *e;* Sight words: *a, and, to, in, no, is, the;*
rd ending: *-s;* Initial consonant blend: *st*

A hen.

A pet hen.

A red pet hen.

A red pet hen gets wet.

A red pet hen begs and begs.

A red pet hen begs to get in bed.

A red pet hen steps in bed.

WET LEGS!

No red pet hen in bed.

A red pet hen is in the pen.

How to Use This Book

Prepare by reading the stories ahead of time.
Familiarize yourself with the skills reinforced in each
story. In doing this, you can better guide your child in
recognizing the new words and sounds as they appear in
the text.

Before reading, look at the pictures with your child.
Encourage him or her to tell the story through the pictures.
Next, read the books aloud to your child. Point to the
words as you read to promote a connection between the
spoken word and the printed word.

Have your child read to you. Encourage him or her to
point to the words as he or she reads. By doing so, your
child will begin to understand that each word has a
separate sound and is represented in a distinct way
on the page.

Encourage your child to read independently. This is
the ultimate goal. Have him or her read alone or read
aloud to other family members and friends.

After You Read Activities

To help reinforce comprehension of the story:
- Ask your child simple questions about the characters, such as "What color is the cat?" (from *Fat Cat*).
- Ask questions that require an understanding of the story, such as "Why is the fat cat glad at the end?"

To reinforce phonetic vowel sounds:
- Ask your child to say words that rhyme with each other and have the same short-vowel sound. For example, *cat, hat,* and *bat*.

To reinforce understanding of words:
- Pick out two or three words from the story and have your child use all of them in a sentence.

To help develop imagination:
- Ask your child to make up a story, using his or her favorite characters from the stories.
- Write the story down so your child can read his or her story later on.
- Have your child draw pictures to go with the story.

The Now I'm Reading!™ Series

The *Now I'm Reading!*™ series integrates the best of phonics and literature-based reading. Phonics emphasizes letter-sound relationships, while a literature-based approach brings the enjoyment and excitement of a real story. The series has six reading levels:

Pre-Reader level: Children "read" simple, patterned, and repetitive text, and use picture clues to help them along.

Level 1: Children learn short vowel sounds, simple consonant sounds, and common sight words.

Level 2: Children learn long and short vowel sounds, more consonants and consonant blends, plus more sight word reinforcement.

Level 3: Children learn new vowel sounds, with more consonant blends, double consonants, and longer words and sentences.

Level 4: Children learn advanced word skills, including silent letters, multi-syllable words, compound words, and contractions.

Independent level: Children are introduced to high-interest topics as they tackle challenging vocabulary words and information by using previous phonics skills.

Glossary of Terms

Phonics: The use of letter-sound relationships to help youngsters identify written words.

Sight Words: Frequently used words, recognized automatically on sight, which do not require decoding, such as *a*, *the*, *is*, and so on.

Decoding: Breaking a word into parts, giving each letter or letter combination its corresponding sound, and then pronouncing the word (sometimes called "sounding out").

Consonant Letters: Letters that represent the consonant sounds and, except *Y*, are not vowels—*B, C, D, F, G, H, J, K, L, M, N, P, Q, R, S, T, V, W, X, Y, Z.*

Short Vowels: The vowel sounds similar to the sound of *a* in *cat*, *o* in *dog*, *i* in *pig*, *u* in *cub*, and *e* in *hen*.

Long Vowels: The vowel sounds that are the same as the names of the alphabet letters *a, e, i, o,* and *u*. Except for *y*, long-vowel words have two vowels in them. They either have a silent *e* at the end of the word (for example *home*), or they use a vowel pattern or combination, such as *ai, ee, ea, oa, ue,* and so on.

Consonant Blend: A sequence of two or more consonants in a word, each of which holds its distinct sound when the word is pronounced. Consonant blends can occur at the beginning or at the end of a word—as in <u>sl</u>ip or la<u>st</u> or <u>str</u>eet.

Consonant Digraph: A combination of two consonant letters that represent a single speech sound, which is different from either consonant sound alone. Consonant digraphs can occur at the beginning or the end of a word—as in <u>sh</u>ip or fi<u>sh</u>.

Literature-Based Reading: Using quality stories and books to help children learn to read.

Reading Comprehension: The ability to understand and integrate information from the text that is read. The skill ranges from a literal understanding of a text to a more critical and creative appreciation of it.

About the Author

Nora Gaydos is an elementary school teacher with more than ten years of classroom experience teaching kindergarten, first grade, and third grade. She has a broad understanding of how beginning readers develop from the earliest stage of pre-reading to becoming independent, self-motivated readers. Nora has a degree in elementary education from Miami University in Ohio and lives in Connecticut with her husband and two sons. Nora is also the author of *Now I Know My ABCs* and *Now I Know My 1, 2, 3's*, as well as other early-learning concept books published by innovative KIDS®.